CHAPTER 1

KING OF THE DINOSAURS

Millions of years ago, Rex was King of the Dinosaurs. He could stomp through all of the swamps he wanted, and none of the Stegosauruses could complain – unless they fancied becoming a delicious brunch. He loved the volcanoes, and the forests, and the football-sized insects... For Rex, this was home.

Then one day, it got cold. Not just a bit chilly: *Ice Age* cold.

And it stayed cold for a long, long time. Millions of years, in fact.

Finally, things started to heat up. As the ice began to crack, one big lump dropped into the sea…

One big lump, containing one big dinosaur.

The iceberg slowly melted as Rex floated across miles of water, until – at last! – land came into view.

But here there were no volcanoes, no forests and not a single massive insect. It was just *scary*. Everywhere he looked, there were predators.

At first, there didn't seem to be anyone to ask for help – but then Rex spotted a couple of friendly faces...

Other dinosaurs! He hurried inside, ready
to ask them what on earth was going on –

only to
discover that this
new place *wasn't*
safe for dinosaurs.
Not. At. All.

What now? There was only one thing Rex

could think to do: hide. He curled up as small as

he could (which wasn't really all that small) –

then suddenly realized how exhausted he was...

Before he knew it, Rex had fallen fast asleep.

Little did he know, as he began to snore, that help *was* close at hand – because Rex wasn't the only one trying to keep a low profile at the museum.

As it happened, Bigfoot had also decided to pay a visit that day. He was careful not to move from his spot in front of one of the museum labels – where he'd been standing for about half an hour. He had seen the other humans do this: they called it "being in the way", and he was confident it only added to his disguise.

Bigfoot had lived in the city for years, and worked hard to disguise himself as the most normal, boring human imaginable. He had built up a wardrobe of beige ties and sensible shirts, found a job in a nearby office and – most enjoyably – he would go on regular day trips to human places, to practise "being in the way".

This was all because he knew exactly what would happen if the humans ever found out he wasn't one of them.

As further protection, Bigfoot had also developed a good sense for when things weren't normal or boring… A sense for when things were about to get a bit too interesting for his liking.

That's why, as he looked around the museum, Bigfoot noticed something the humans – distracted by the displays – hadn't yet noticed.

There was one dinosaur that wasn't just a bunch of bones. And it was asleep behind a pot plant.

Is that a human in a dinosaur costume? That's an odd place for a nap.

Bigfoot thought, while pretending to be engrossed in his map.

Wait a second! Could it be... ?

At that moment, the dinosaur jolted awake and saw Bigfoot looking at him.

"Rargh?" said Rex, sounding hopeful.

Yep, thought Bigfoot. *That is* definitely *not a human.*

What was he going to do? He could hardly just leave the dinosaur here, waiting for the humans to ship him off to a zoo. And what if they started looking for other "dangerous creatures"?

No, Bigfoot decided. *I have to do something.*

He kneeled down next to the shivering dinosaur. "It's OK," he said. "I'm here to help. Just stay still for a moment – I need to make you look human." He passed Rex the museum map,

took a scarf from his backpack and wrapped
it around the dinosaur's neck, then carefully
perched his spare pair of glasses onto Rex's snout.

"Come on," he said, straightening up. "We'd
better go back to my flat – you'll be safe there."

He reached out a hairy hand, helping Rex
to his feet.

"You've got a lot to learn about the human
world," Bigfoot told him. "But, lucky for you,
I know a thing or two about 'Being Human'."

CHAPTER 2
BEING HUMAN

R ex had learnt a lot in the space of a few short hours. The hairy man, known as "Bigfoot", had given him a crash course in "speaking" (a more complicated type of roaring used by humans). That was how Rex had learned that his name wasn't pronounced "RAAAOOOEEERRR" here – just "Rex".

Then Bigfoot had told Rex that he was about to meet what he called his "friends".

"I'm Dodo," said the small, feathery one, "but you can call me Mr Dodo."

"And I'm Nessy," said the long, thin one.

Rex gave Nessy a puzzled look. "Are you a dinosaur?"

Nessy thought about this. "If I'm honest, I'm not sure – but I dinnae think I need to be labelled."

Rex was still making sense of this, when his attention was caught by something else. Something ... wonderful.

Bigfoot had set a big bag on the table, labelled "Cheez Nubbins". Rex had never smelled anything quite like Cheez Nubbins in prehistoric times... Or seen anything remotely as orange.

"Can I eat these?" asked Rex, tearing his eyes away from the Nubbins bag to look at Bigfoot.

"Only if you listen very carefully to what we have to say," said Bigfoot.

Dodo gave an impatient flap of his wings. "Shall we get on with this, young Foot? I don't have all day – I've got a small but profitable restaurant to run!"

While Rex wondered what exactly a "small but profitable restaurant" might be, Bigfoot cleared his throat.

"Ahem! So, Rex, we've got some very important things to tell you," he announced. "Fortunately, the humans have the perfect method for delivering important information. Behold: the computer slideshow!"

Nessy and Dodo groaned as Bigfoot spun the laptop

BIGFOOT PRESENTS
UNDERCOVER
CREATURES

around to face them, but Rex was transfixed by the light coming from the screen – and tried to give it a tentative lick.

"No thank you!" said Bigfoot, pulling the laptop away. "I see we'll have to cover 'What Is and Isn't Food' at some point." He cleared his throat a second time for good measure, and began: "Thank you, everyone, for coming to my presentation 'How to Be an Undercover Creature Living in the City'." He turned to Rex. "These days, Rex, the world is run by creatures called 'humans'."

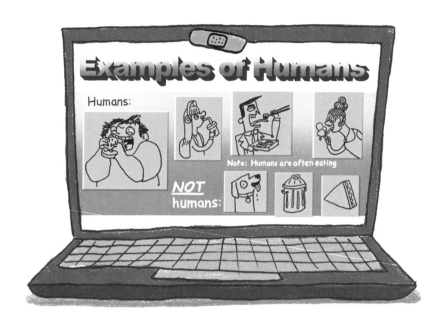

Rex inspected the presentation slide closely.

"OK ... and could I be friends with the humans?"

"NO!" shouted all three creatures.

"Nothing is more dangerous than a human, young Rex!" said Dodo, looking horrified. "Do you want to know why I went into the restaurant trade?"

"Restau-RAAARGH?" said Rex.

Dodo continued as if he hadn't heard.

"Back in olden times, the humans ate every

single dodo they could find – apparently, we're delicious. My family were the only ones with enough sense to hide, so the humans think we're extinct." His feathers were ruffled with indignation. "That's why I set up my restaurant chain: Dodo Burger. If you don't want humans eating you, you've gotta keep them well fed."

"Aye," said Nessy, "dinnae underestimate the humans. They're the reason I had to leave Scotland: they got obsessed with hanging around my loch and trying to take my photo without my permission."

"I had to get out of there," she continued, "and I've been working as a lifeguard at the swimming pool, here in the city, ever since. But I still miss home."

Rex understood about missing home. He didn't know how he was going to manage in this new place full of dangerous humans, trying to take his photo, and eat him, and—

Bigfoot gave a cough. "Thanks for that, Dodo and Nessy. So you understand, Rex, there's a whole LOAD of humans that want to do bad things to unusual creatures like us."

Rex was wide-eyed. "That sounds –" he struggled to find the word – "big not good. Lots of not good?"

"Bad," Bigfoot supplied. "That's why Dodo and Nessy have to pretend that they're normal, boring humans, and stay undercover … and it's the same for me, too." He clicked to the next slide. "I used to live in the mountains with the rest of the yetis – it was very different to the city, and it wasn't really for me."

"It's much better here in the city," continued Bigfoot, polishing his glasses on his furry arm. "All the humans think I'm a normal human guy called 'Brian', who works in an office and likes jazz."

"That's right," said Dodo, "and the humans call ME 'Mr Dodo', and think I'm just a very successful local businessman."

"Aye, and they call me 'Vanessa' and won't stop running at the side of ma pool," said Nessy.

"*Ahem.* That brings me to the last section," said Bigfoot. He put on his glasses to check over a piece of paper, before handing it to Rex. "This is a list of human rules to follow."

Rex read through the rules carefully – they didn't seem too tricky.

RULES

① Humans wear shirts, ties, trousers, pants UNDER trousers and socks on the endy bits.

② Humans look at their phones A LOT.

③ Humans talk about human things, like the weather, late trains and funny cats on the internet.

④ Humans drink loads of coffee.

⑤ Humans ARE ALWAYS EATING!

In fact, after giving it a go, Rex thought he might just have this whole human thing covered…

Bigfoot seemed to think his undercover
look still needed a bit of work, though. And
they'd have to sort it out fast – because the
time had come to put Rex's disguise to the test.

CHAPTER 3
SANDRA SHELLMAN

Not far away from where Rex was learning the ropes, there lived a girl called Sandra Shellman. Sandra's home was the flat below Bigfoot's, which she shared with her mum, dad and three new baby brothers, Larry, Gary and Barry. It was a bit of a squish.

At nine-and-a-third years old, Sandra had grown up in the city and was quite an expert on its strange, and even *supernatural*, goings-on.

But on the day of Rex's arrival, she was trying to solve an altogether different kind of mystery.

Sandra peeped her head around the door of her brothers' room, where her parents were dealing with what they referred to as DEFCON 3: Brown Alert. (This was when all three of the triplets' nappies needed changing at once.)

"Mum, Dad… Can I ask you something?" Sandra leaned on the door frame and shuffled her feet.

"As long as it's quick, sweetie," said Sandra's mum, grabbing an alarmingly large handful of wet wipes.

Sandra took a deep breath. "It's about Maddie," she told them. "Something's happened: she's stopped being my friend. And not just my *best* friend … she's stopped being my friend at all."

Maddie and Sandra had met on their first day of school, and bonded straight away over their shared love of all things mysterious: aliens, ghosts, invisible people, alligators living in the drains... There was ALWAYS something to investigate.

That is, until something changed.

"First she stopped talking to me, which was bad enough," Sandra continued, "but then she made friends with these other girls… Hannah M, the one with light-up trainers, and Hannah P, the one with the purple lip gloss. Now, whenever I see Maddie, they all look at me and start giggling."

"That's *not* a nice way to behave," said Dad, as he threw a nappy at the bin. (It missed.)

"Why would things change, just like that?" Sandra wondered aloud. "Do you think it's … ALIENS?"

"Sometimes people change," said Mum, who seemed to be ignoring the bit about aliens. "What about Anish, is he your friend?"

"Sort of, but Maddie's the one I do the mystery investigations with. I don't understand what happened… How do I find out? Do you think I can change her back?"

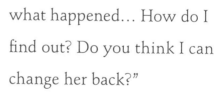

Mum waggled a squishy giraffe toy to distract Barry, who had started to grizzle. "Have you tried talking to her, Sandra?"

"She barely even looks at me, Mum, especially with those other girls around. I thought UFOs were her thing," said Sandra, staring down at her own spaceship-patterned socks. "It's like they've brainwashed her with ponies and dance routines."

The giraffe hadn't worked: Barry went from a grizzle into a full-blown wail.

"Oh no, here we go," said Dad, as Barry's crying started Larry off, which, in turn, set Gary off. "WE'LL TALK ABOUT IT LATER, HONEY," he continued, over the crying.

"YOU'LL HAVE TO ENTERTAIN YOURSELF FOR NOW," added Mum.

Sandra closed the bedroom door, which didn't dampen the crying much. She couldn't help but wonder whether *anyone* really wanted her around: not Maddie, and not even Mum and Dad when they were so busy with the boys.

She needed to take her mind off things, and it was impossible in the flat, with the triplets screaming the place down.

Sandra stepped out onto the landing … and spotted their neighbour, Mr Foot, on the way up the stairs to his flat. Behind him was someone she'd never seen before.

"Hi, Mr Foot," she called. "Who's that?"

Mr Foot looked down at Sandra. "Ummm, hello… Well … er… This is my friend, Mr… Ummm…"

"Rex! That's my name now. Greetings, small human!" Mr Rex gave Sandra an enthusiastic wave – then whispered to Mr Foot, easily loud enough for Sandra to hear, "I spoke to a human AND remembered how to say my name!"

You did really well, Rex. The humans had no idea.

Sandra raised an eyebrow and followed them to Mr Foot's door. Grown-ups were often odd, but this was something different.

Mr Foot fumbled in his pocket and pulled out his keys. "Erm, yes! Mr Rex has just moved to the city from – errr – far, far away. He's a bit new to things."

He moved for his door, but before he could reach it, Mr Rex got there instead … and leaned over and bit the door handle.

Mr Foot looked at Sandra. "He's had a very long flight, as you can see."

Sandra watched as he prised Mr Rex off the door handle. She could have sworn she heard Mr Foot say, "Now that's not how we do it in the city, we use our hands because we're all humans here!", but before she had time to think, Mr Foot had opened the door and hustled Mr Rex inside.

"Nice to see you, Sandra," he called over his shoulder. "Say 'hi' to your mum and dad."

"Bye, Mr Foot and Mr ... Rex?" said Sandra.

The door shut with a click.

Well! thought Sandra. *There's* something *mysterious going on here.*

And that could only mean one thing: she was going to have to investigate.

CHAPTER 4
MONEY

The next morning, Bigfoot pushed a little metal disc towards Rex.

"Another very important human thing you have to learn about, Rex, is money," he announced. He reached into his pocket and took out a paper rectangle – and some more, very shiny, discs.

"Ooooh, sparkly!" said Rex, picking up a disc with his claws. "What are they for – looking nice? And can I keep this one? I've just learned about 'having things', and I think this is a thing I'd like to have."

Bigfoot took it off him. "No and no. This is a 'coin', Rex, and this –" he waved the paper rectangle – "is a 'note'. They're 'money', and you can swap them for things in shops."

"Shops?" asked Rex.

"A shop is one of those houses you're allowed to go inside," Bigfoot told him, "where they have all the stuff on shelves. Like Mike's News and Lotto on the corner."

"Oh, yeah!" Rex nodded. "That's where you got the Cheez Nubbins from! So *this* is how you get Nubbins? And also news? What is Lotto?"

"Lotto is not for you."

"Let's swap ALL the money for Cheez Nubbins!"

said Rex, in his outside voice.

"Please stop shouting or the neighbours will hear." Bigfoot kept glancing at the door, as if he thought his neighbours would come and bang it down at any minute. "And no, we can't swap these – it would buy too many Nubbins. You can swap the paper ones for more stuff than the shiny ones: they're worth more."

Rex screwed up his face. "The shiny ones are more interesting. Shouldn't they be worth more Nubbins?"

"That's just not how it works," said Bigfoot. "The numbers tell you how much it's worth."

"Numbers?" said Rex, and looked around the room, as if "numbers" might jump out at him from behind the sofa.

"Oh dear: I haven't explained numbers yet, have I?" said Bigfoot. "No time now, though, I have to go to work. We'll do them later... And you better take this, Rex, in case you need it."

Bigfoot handed Rex a shiny blue rectangle.

"This is like money, but not," he told Rex, whose head was starting to ache. "If you have to buy something, just hold this near the paying machine and it goes **BEEP!** That means you're  allowed to take whatever it is you want home."

"I like how it's blue," said Rex, holding it very close to his eye.

"That's my Careful Savers Premium Card. They don't hand them out to any old human, you know." Bigfoot puffed up his chest.

"Now just stay quiet while I'm at work – and remember, only use the card in an *emergency*."

With that, Bigfoot grabbed his briefcase and shut the door behind him.

"What's an 'emergency'?" Rex asked the empty flat.

After a few hours left to his own devices, Rex wasn't sure what he was supposed to be doing. He'd tried hunting for Stegosauruses, but there didn't seem to be any in the flat – not even in the bathroom.

OK
↓

To pass the time, Rex had eaten all the remaining Nubbins (*delicious*), a block of Edam (*OK*), a bar of soap (*yuck!*) and a pot plant (*Stegosaurus food*). But he was still hungry, so he grabbed the blue card and – after tangling with the confusing door again – Went Shopping.

The Best
↑

← awful!

bad →

51

That evening, Bigfoot opened the flat door and dropped his single shopping bag on the doormat.

"Rex, I'm home! I popped to the supermarket and I'm going to make something called 'lasagne' for dinner, which I think you're going to like—"

That was when Bigfoot noticed the bags dumped in the hallway: lots and LOTS of bags. There was at least one from every shop on the high street... The supermarket, the chemist, the DIY store, the pound shop, and – worst of all – Harknell and Lefroy's, the fancy shop for fancy people!

In the living room, he discovered even MORE bags, stuffed with all sorts of random things: golf clubs, a beach ball, a sack of

onions, six pairs of prescription glasses, quite a lot of gaffer tape and a rather interesting sculpture of a horse.

In the middle of it all was Rex, working his way through one of what were easily twenty family-sized bags of Cheez Nubbins.

"REX!" Bigfoot began pulling things out of bags with increasing horror. "This is much more stuff than any normal human needs!"

"No shouting, Bigfoot, remember?" said Rex, getting crumbs from the Cheez Nubbins all over the floor. "I used the blue money rectangle to get us things. I found **LOTS** of shops! Did you know there were so many?"

"We can't afford all this stuff!"

"But look," said Rex, reaching into one of the bags, "you can get a little me!"

Triumphantly, he stuck a plastic dinosaur under Bigfoot's nose.

"And that's not all." Rex started rummaging through a bag. "Here's a little *you*!"

He thrust a stuffed toy into Bigfoot's arms.

"That is NOT a little me," said Bigfoot, holding the toy away from himself. "That is a cuddly orang-utan ... and it's not even the right colour. That's actually quite rude."

All the excitement drained out of Rex. "Are you not happy? I thought I was doing really well at money – I wore my disguise the whole time, and I didn't do any Lotto, and I was acting just like a real human in the shops. They were all beeping their rectangles."

Bigfoot let out a big sigh and flopped down to sit on the empty Nubbins packets. He tried to think back to his first week in the city, and how confusing he'd found water fountains and pet shops and all the other new things.

"I get it, Rex," he said at last. "You tried your best – and some of this IS good stuff. Your new tie is very ... unconventional."

Rex gave his rainbow-spotty tie a proud pat with his claw.

"But you went a little over the top," Bigfoot continued. "We don't have the money to buy all this. We have to be careful so we don't run out."

"Even the rectangle runs out? But it still looks the same as it did this morning," said Rex. "Can I get more money to fill it up again?"

"Yes – you *can* get more money, Rex," said Bigfoot, tapping his chin thoughtfully. "And I think it's time that you found out how."

STOMP!

CHAPTER 5

THE INVESTIGATION

A lot of noise had been coming from upstairs. Sandra was familiar with all the normal noises you heard in flats: the sound of pipes rattling, for example, or the **BANG** of doors slamming… Or the constant barking of her neighbour Mrs Mince's dog (which never, *ever* stopped yapping). But this was different.

Another **STOMP** and **RAAAOORR** from the ceiling made up her mind – Sandra strode into the kitchen.

"Mum, Dad," said Sandra, "I think I need to start an investigation, even if I have to do it without Maddie." She tried hard not to think about how excited the *old* Maddie would have been about having a new mystery to solve.

"Sandra Jane Shellman, do NOT tell me you're planning on spying on the neighbours again." Sandra's mum was busy trying to persuade Gary to wear his bib.

"But you don't get it, Mum – there are some REALLY WEIRD noises coming from upstairs."

"What even *is* a weird noise, when you live in the city?" said Dad, through his bowl of Wheat O' Hoops. "This is just what living in flats is like, Sandra."

A big wail – not unlike a dinosaur roar –
started coming out of Larry.

"Something's set Larry off again. I need
to deal with this before the others start." Dad
scooped up Larry and headed for the bedroom.

Sandra turned back to Mum. "Will you
come and listen, just for a second? You'd see
what I mean, then – and maybe we could …
do the investigation together?"

Mum reached over and gave Sandra's hand
a squeeze (which was nice, although Sandra
couldn't help but find the baby breakfast in her
mum's hair a little distracting).

"I'm sorry, honey," she said, "but I just
haven't got time – and *you've* got to go to
school. We'll do something together soon, I
promise. For now, I just need you to be a good
girl and NOT annoy the neighbours."

Sandra tried not to look as hurt as she felt
… but there was nothing for it.

She'd have to go it alone.

One night, when her parents were out and
the babysitter had fallen asleep, Sandra had
watched a police show – so she knew
that if you wanted to find something out about a suspect, you
just had to look in their bins.
That was where all the best
evidence would be: clues,
fingerprints and DNA.

(Sandra wasn't totally
sure what DNA was,
but she supposed she'd
know it when she
saw it.)

As soon as Sandra got home from school that day, she headed straight for Mr Foot's rubbish in the alley behind the flats…

But she'd barely begun to investigate, when she saw *them*. Maddie and the Hannahs were right there, walking down the road!

For a split second, Sandra hesitated; then she called out: "Maddie? I've got something I have to tell you about!"

At first she didn't think Maddie could have heard her, because there was no reply. But then Sandra heard another voice.

"Hey, Mads, isn't that the Shellman girl you used to hang around with?" It was Hannah P. "What's she doing in that bin?"

"Let's just keep moving." This time it was Maddie, but her voice was hard to hear.

"No, that's really weird. I want to see what she's doing."

Hannah P appeared at the end of the alleyway, then began marching towards Sandra; Hannah M and Maddie followed closely after, although Maddie didn't seem particularly happy about it.

Sandra was starting to think attracting the attention of the Hannahs might not have been such a good idea… But she so wanted to believe that her old Maddie was still in there – and she couldn't resist giving it another try.

"Maddie, you won't believe what's going on with my new neighbour. I know you've not been into this stuff recently, but I think we've got a real-life mystery on our hands."

She pointed at the hundreds of empty Cheez Nubbins packets, spread all across the bottom of the bin.

"Look at this!"

But Maddie only frowned at Sandra.

"Ewww!" said Hannah P. "Have you been going through your neighbours' rubbish? That's disgusting! Isn't it, Mads?"

Still, Maddie said nothing.

Sandra was starting to feel really nervous now, but she decided to have one last go – after all, they finally had a real mystery to solve! How could she make Maddie *see*?

"If you just had a look at some of the stuff in the bin..." she began.

"I don't want to play these games any more, Sandra!" Maddie had finally decided to speak, and she sounded furious. "Looking for stuff in bins is weird."

"AND it's just 'ew'," added Hannah M.

Sandra flinched. "But you don't understand—"

"SHUT UP, Sandra!"

Maddie scowled at her.

"Try being *normal* for once."

The Hannahs burst out laughing.

"Why don't we give you a hand with your bin-diving?" said Hannah P.

"You can give her a PUSH in the right direction, Mads."

"Yeah!" said Hannah M, and started to chant: "In-the-bin. In-the-bin! IN-THE-BIN!"

"IN-THE-BIN!" Hannah P joined in.

Maddie looked at Sandra, and Sandra looked back at Maddie from her precarious position on top of the bin.

"Maddie," said Sandra, "please, you don't have to—"

But as the Hannahs cheered her on, Maddie gave Sandra a quick, hard push.

Fortunately, Cheez Nubbins packets make for a soft landing. Sandra lay as still as she could in the bottom of the bin, listening to the fading giggles of Maddie's new friends as they left the alley.

She could feel tears starting to squeeze their way from her eyes, but she knew she had to keep her mind on the job. Maddie might not care, but there *was* a mystery here.

And after a quick examination of what she'd landed on, it was clear Sandra was going to need a new investigation partner – because she would need help to figure out what on earth could leave such gigantic bite marks...

CHAPTER 6
OFFICE JOB

A couple of days later, Bigfoot hustled Rex onto a bus headed into the city, with stern instructions to sit still and act human.

When the bus set off, he turned to face Rex. "To survive in the human world, Rex," he said, "you need to get a job."

Rex gave him a puzzled look.

"A 'job' is when you do things for someone, and they give you money in return," Bigfoot explained.

Rex seemed to brighten. "I can do things! And then we'll fill up the rectangle again?"

"Yes," said Bigfoot approvingly. "I work at an office called BusinessCorp – I'm the Senior Printer Operator. I've got you a job as a Junior Pencil Sharpener."

"What things will I do?" asked Rex. "I can stomp and roar very well."

"Your job is mainly going to be to do with pencils. But don't worry," said Bigfoot, giving Rex a grin, "I've prepared another presentation to explain everything."

Rex pulled a face. "Is it like the last one?"

"Oh, no," said Bigfoot. "This one's MUCH longer."

Upon their arrival, it became clear to Rex that an "office" was a huge grey box. Inside the box were lots of grey-looking humans – and Bigfoot directed Rex past the humans into another, smaller grey box, called a "conference room".

He passed Rex a notepad and pencil. "Pay close attention, Rex, because this office is very important to me."

He stepped back, and pointed to a picture of a fierce-looking human.

"Andrea's the boss," Bigfoot began. "Think of her as the top dinosaur: the most dangerous predator. The main thing to remember is that you *can't* make me look bad in front of her – because I think I'm on track for a big promotion." He smiled proudly.

"A 'promo-show'?" said Rex.

"It's when they give you a better job and pay you more money," Bigfoot told him.

"Oh – to buy more Nubbins."

Bigfoot ignored him. "You just have to follow a few simple rules – the first being that you need to keep your head down.

Rex leaned down and put his head between his legs.

"No, Rex, not your actual head. What I mean is, you need to act

74

like a boring human and not attract attention to yourself. Are you taking all this down?"

"Mm-hmm," said Rex.

"What next? Oh, yes! Another essential part of office life is the break room."

Bigfoot led Rex to another small grey box-room. "This is it: when it's time for lunch, this is the place where you go to eat it."

"Lunch?" asked Rex.

"Middle-of-the-day-food, like sandwiches."

"Oh, yes!" said Rex. "The bread towers. The humans should really make those taller."

Bigfoot ignored him again. "You can also make a tea or coffee in here. Remember – you

need to drink coffees to seem human, so

we should probably make one now. Do you remember how?"

Rex nodded enthusiastically. He'd been practising making coffee and it was time to impress Bigfoot by remembering all the steps. He opened one of the cupboards (he was getting better at doors) and it revealed shelves full of mugs. Rex saw the perfect one...

"No!" Bigfoot swiped his claw away. "DON'T touch the one with the dinosaur! That belongs to Sean from Accounting."

Rex reached for another.

"No, DON'T touch the 'I Hate Mondays' one!" said Bigfoot. "That belongs to Darnell from Sales."

Rex tried again.

"No, DON'T touch the 'Kitten
Fiend' one!" Bigfoot shook his head.
"That belongs to Nigel from IT."

Before Rex could try another
mug, they were interrupted by a human.

"Brian, there you are!" she said. "Where
have you been? There's a printer emergency
down on the third floor."

"Hi, Maggie," said Bigfoot, sounding
distracted. "I'm just showing the new guy the
ropes, so I can't—"

"Andrea said you should take care of it
personally. People are getting paper cuts!" the
human – "Maggie" – told him.

Bigfoot looked at Rex, and Rex looked at
Bigfoot. Rex wasn't sure about being
left alone with the office humans,
and Bigfoot seemed on edge too.

Rex saw Bigfoot take a big breath, before he said, "Rex, you just stay here until I'm back, OK? Don't go anywhere … just make that coffee."

And with that, Bigfoot went striding off.

Maggie brightened up. "Oh, are you making coffees, New Guy?" she said. "I'll have one if you don't mind, and Darren in Customer Services was after one too."

"If you've got the kettle on, I'll have a latte!" yelled one of the humans behind her.

"And me!" yelled another.

Rex stared at all the mugs he wasn't allowed to touch. He was going to have to use some of this "thinking" Bigfoot was always going on about, to get all these humans their coffee without using the forbidden mugs.

Fortunately, he had an idea.

"Good job with the printer, Brian," said Andrea as, some time later, she and Bigfoot made their way towards the break room. "I have no idea how Norman from Appliances caught his ear in it, but you saved the day. You've shown a lot of potential recently, and I've been thinking—"

Andrea stopped in her tracks.

"Wait... WHO is THAT?"

Bigfoot spotted Rex through the desks – and his new system for delivering coffee.

"Brian, get the new guy in my office right now!" said Andrea, and marched off.

Bigfoot felt dread in the pit of his stomach. This was NOT how you kept your head down and acted like a nice, boring office human.

He fetched Rex and led him to Andrea's office, expecting the worst.

"Does Andrea want a coffee too?" asked Rex, sounding puzzled.

"No," said Bigfoot, who was starting to sweat. "Just sit quietly and listen."

Inside the office, Andrea gestured for Rex to sit – and he squeezed into the chair opposite her desk.

"So, New Guy, this coffee fountain... You realize this isn't normal office procedure?"

"He didn't mean to do anything wrong—" Bigfoot started to explain.

"Because I think it's GENIUS!" continued Andrea, leaving Bigfoot with his mouth hanging open. "Coffee straight to the desks: so good for morale and productivity! No

workers wasting time, getting up to go to the kitchen..." She beamed at Rex. "I like your style, New Guy. What's your name?"

"Rex!" Rex smiled and waved.

"Rex, we should really play golf

some time. But for now, I've been looking to promote someone to Office Manager – and I think you'd be perfect. How about it?"

Rex lit up. "Yes, of course, Mrs Business." He turned to look at Bigfoot. "A promo-show!"

Bigfoot's eyes widened. That was the promotion *he* wanted: he had been working towards it for months, acting as human as he could. Rex had been there for one day, done one weird thing and snatched that promotion away from him! It just didn't seem fair…

At that moment, Maggie rushed in through the door. "Sorry to interrupt, guys, but the printer's at it again – and this time, it's got Norman's whole head!"

"I thought you fixed that, Brian," said Andrea, rising from her large leather chair. "We'd better get down there. Rex, you're in charge; keep at it with the coffee and whatever other time-saving initiatives you can think of. Just think BIGGER and BETTER!"

Bigfoot silently fumed, but – with a forced smile at Rex – he obediently followed Andrea out of the office to extract Norman's head from the printer.

Meanwhile, Rex was feeling very proud – Bigfoot had said a promo-show meant more money. That would solve their problems.

Bigfoot was going to be so pleased with him! Now he had to figure out how to be an Office Manager. Good thing Andrea had given him such clear instructions: he just had to do things BIGGER and BETTER ... and all Rex did around here was make coffee. So, while Andrea and Bigfoot were busy with the printer, and the other office humans were taking a long lunch, Rex put the kettle on and got to work.

Andrea is going to love this, thought Rex.

If that wasn't BIGGER and BETTER, Rex didn't know what was. He gave Bigfoot an excited wave as he walked back onto the office floor.

At first, Bigfoot seemed excited too: he raised his hands to his head and rushed over to Rex.

But then, he started shouting:

"Oh MY GOSH, REX!

What have you done?! First you take my promotion, then you turn the office into a coffee swimming pool… Andrea is going to sack us **BOTH**!"

Rex stared blankly as Bigfoot seethed. This was all *very* confusing.

"I did the coffee BIGGER and BETTER, Bigfoot, just like Andrea said. But if you don't like it, I can clean it up! It will all be gone in a second."

He picked up a recycling bin full of coffee and started rapidly gulping it down.

"No, Rex, don't clean it up like that!" said Bigfoot. "If you drink that much coffee, that fast, it'll make you—"

Rex suddenly stopped gulping. His eyes opened wide and his cheeks bulged, until – with a huge and spectacular "BLEURGH!" – Rex ejected all of the coffee across the office.

Unfortunately, it was at this exact moment that Andrea walked in.

New guy! You are **FIRED!**

CHAPTER 7

PE

Meanwhile, at Lower Patterson Primary School, everyone's least favourite lesson was underway: PE. The reason it was so unpopular had to do with the PE teacher, Mrs Libson.

"COME ON, YOU LOT! YOU CAN JUMP HIGHER THAN THAT!" yelled Mrs Libson.

Mrs Libson didn't like children much – in fact, she only really seemed to like two things. The first was making her class do star jumps, and the second was 4B's class guinea pig ... which she had taken to perching on her shoulder like a pirate's parrot.

"Isn't that right, my fluffy-wuffy darling?" she continued, blowing the guinea pig a kiss.

Sandra had no problem with people liking guinea pigs, but Mrs Libson had taken things to a bit of an extreme.

Right now though, Sandra had more important things on her mind than the PE teacher: she needed to talk to Anish. Subtly, she began to star-jump her way across the hall to where Anish was leaping with all his might.

"Anish," hissed Sandra, still jumping, "I need your help."

"Right … *puff* … now?" Anish was sweating.

"Yes!" Between jumps Sandra explained about Maddie, their investigations and her mysterious new neighbour. "So, I need a new investigation partner," she said finally. "And, well ... a friend."

Sandra stopped jumping – and found that she felt a bit nervous. What if Anish didn't care, just like Maddie?

Anish stopped jumping too, and bent over to catch his breath. "Do you REALLY think this 'Mr Rex' guy isn't human?"

"I'm sure of it. I just need to figure out what he actually is," said Sandra. "I'm thinking maybe a badly programmed robot?"

"Could be," said Anish, looking thoughtful. "Anyway... What exactly *happened* with Maddie? I saw she wasn't hanging out with you any more."

They both looked across the hall at Maddie. Maddie glanced up and, for a moment, everyone's eyes met – before they all turned away, pretending no one had been staring.

"That's a whole other mystery," said Sandra. "So ... are you up for investigating Mr Rex?"

Anish pretended to consider for a moment, then grinned. "Of course! And as for the friends thing – goes without saying, doesn't it? Although I guess I've just gone and said it, now."

Anish bumped Sandra's fist, and she let out a breath she hadn't realized she'd been holding.

"We'll need code names," said Sandra. "I'll be ... 'Big Spider'."

Mrs Libson had spotted their momentary lack of jumping. **"SANDRA SHELLMAN! ANISH CHANDA!** THOSE ARE NOT STAR JUMPS! Are they, my sweet piggy-pig?"

They started half-heartedly jumping again, but Mrs Libson was clearly not satisfied.

"NONE OF THESE JUMPS ARE HIGH ENOUGH, FAST ENOUGH, OR SPARKLY ENOUGH! I'll show you how it's done."

And she began to demonstrate:

Without a second's pause, the PE teacher
ran for the window and dove out after the
guinea pig. "MR FLUFFEEEEEEEEEE!" she
wailed – and then, Mrs Libson was gone.

"They're OK," yelled one of the children, who had rushed over to the window. "Good thing we're on the ground floor."

But moments later, everyone could hear the stern voice of the head teacher, Mr Alfreds, and Mrs Libson's snappish but defeated-sounding reply.

"Sounds like we're going to need to find a new PE teacher," said Anish. "But that's decided my new codename... Call me 'Flying Pig'."

Author's Note: **In case you're still worried about 4B's guinea pig, the worst it suffered was a stubbed toe ... but it still insisted on being admitted to the animal hospital, probably just to get away from Mrs Libson. 4B went to visit it on a school trip.**

It did later decide to retire from being a class pet, and now lives with Gareth from 4B in a luxury detached hutch – but it doesn't *keep in touch* with 4B's former PE teacher.

Squee!

GET WELL
SOON

Love 4B

Author's Note to the Author's Note: *Mrs Libson was also absolutely fine, but hasn't attempted a star jump since.*

CHAPTER 8

SWIMMING

Rex had just found out about swimming pools. He'd never been keen on the real sea because of the waves – and also all the Liopleurodons trying to eat him. But this little inside version was the perfect solution.

Still, Rex would have been a lot more excited about the pool if things hadn't gone so badly with Bigfoot the night before.

While Bigfoot had calmed down a lot after realizing he wouldn't get fired, Rex could tell he was still angry – and maybe a bit sad, too – even if he was trying hard not to be.

Rex had really wanted to make things better, so he took a deep breath and just came out with it: "I am very bad and I feel like I am bad but I want you to not feel bad any more."

"The word you're looking for is 'sorry'," said Bigfoot.

"I'm a very big sorry. Shall I bring you some Cheez Nubbins?" Rex grinned hopefully.

Bigfoot looked at Rex, then stared down at his very large slippers. "It's OK, Rex," he said, after a pause. "I guess you've learned things from this, at least… Like how you shouldn't cover your boss in coffee puke." He reached for his phone. "I'll call Nessy: there are always jobs going at the leisure centre."

And *that* was how Rex found himself stood by Nessy, at the edge of the pool.

"NAE RUNNING BY THE POOL!" *WEEEEEEEEE!* Nessy blew her whistle as children rushed past, then turned to Rex. "As lifeguards, it's our job to watch the pool and make sure everyone stays safe."

Rex considered this. Maybe he could be a good guard: he did have a knack for warding off predators.

"You've got three things to remember," said Nessy. "Nae splashing, nae running and nae diving. And if you see anyone in trouble, it's your job to help. If in doubt, blow your whistle – that's what I do."

Nessy gave another blast of her whistle, and Rex nodded vigorously.

"Now, go and get your trunks on."

Rex wasn't sure about the swimming trunks, but being a lifeguard didn't seem too difficult. He stood at the side of the pool, guarding, while Nessy swam about and occasionally shouted at swimmers.

"NAE SPLASHING!" yelled Nessy.

"NO RUNNING!" Rex shouted back.

"Very good," said Nessy approvingly. "You seem like you're getting the hang of this, Rex."

Rex blew his whistle in response.

"Great job. I'm going to take my break now. You watch the pool and make sure everyone behaves."

After a quick look around to make sure no one was watching, Nessy dived under the water, swam down through the pool drain ... and disappeared.

Rex settled himself into the lifeguard chair and surveyed the pool. Everything seemed in order. He blew his whistle, just to make sure.

But then he heard something – a big **GGGRRRLLLL** sound, coming from his stomach. It sounded like an angry Allosaurus.

If only he'd brought a snack! Snacking was one of his favourite human activities and he was getting very good at it.

Then Rex remembered something he had seen in the lobby of the leisure centre.

A snack rectangle!

Bigfoot had told him that, if you put the round money in the slot, the rectangle would give you food. And Rex had some round money, because he wasn't allowed to use the money card any more.

Rex could run and get the Nubbins from the rectangle before anyone even noticed he was gone – it was the perfect plan!

It took Rex a bit of time to solve the button-pushing puzzle on the front of the machine. He got his Cheez Nubbins in the end, but he did accidentally buy a Chocosquelch bar, a bag of Chilli Puffs and a cherry-flavoured juice box, too.

He gathered them all up in his little arms and hurried back to the pool as fast as he could... But when he got back, Rex didn't like what he saw.

Rex was going to have to restore order before Nessy came back. He tried all the things she had suggested ...

but they didn't seem to do the trick.

Then Rex spotted a much bigger problem.
A predator had captured one of the human
children! He had to act fast.

Rex hit the water and splashed about, trying to find the predator. But then something important occurred to him: he'd never been swimming before. In fact, he didn't know How To Swim. The humans had made it look so easy!

He waved his arms, legs and tail around as much as he could, but he just got all mixed up underneath the water. The harder he tried, the more he seemed to sink down – and down – and down. He started to panic—

Then Rex felt human hands, grabbing him and pulling him upwards; he burst through the surface of the pool, flopping onto the edge…

Which was when Nessy came back from her break.

"There's water everywhere!" She looked furious. "What did I tell ye about splashing, Rex? You've broken the pool rules!"

BURGER

CHAPTER 9
LE CHEF

After the disaster at the pool, Bigfoot and Rex dropped in at Dodo Burger to wallow in their feelings.

"I'll never be able to show my face at the leisure centre again," said Bigfoot. "You can't keep making such a mess of these jobs, Rex, it's just … not very human."

"Could I have one more job?" Rex offered Bigfoot a Dodo Nuggit hopefully. "I promise I'll act really human this time."

At that moment, Dodo came waddling over. "I couldn't help but overhear, young Rex, and I think I can help. I need an assistant for a catering job today… Can you fill in?"

Rex perked up. "Can I, Bigfoot?"

Bigfoot hesitated for a moment, then shrugged. "OK, if you're on your best behaviour – just remember to act human, Rex."

Rex barely had time to wave goodbye before Dodo had hustled him into something called a "taxi". It felt like seconds later, when they arrived in a building even larger than Bigfoot's office – and he followed Dodo until they reached a huge room full of bright lights, strange boxes and very busy humans.

"What's happening, Mr Dodo? Is this my new job?" said Rex.

"That it is, young Rex!" replied Dodo. "I'm going to be on TV, talking about my All-New-Low-Fat-Burgerless-Burger."

Rex knew all about TV: it was the loud picture in the living room, full of tiny, moving humans.

"You're going to be my assistant," Dodo continued. "All celebrities have assistants."

A woman with a clipboard spotted Rex and Dodo and started hurrying over.

"Thank God you're here." The woman shook Rex's claw and Dodo's wing. "I'm Lauren, the producer. We're having a nightmare today: our other guest dropped out. Now we don't have a chef for the cookery segment!"

"Oh dear ... you must be desperate for a replacement," said Dodo, raising a feathery eyebrow. "Was this chef very famous?"

"Yes! Incredibly famous," said Lauren.

"So you were paying them a lot?"

"Yes, loads!"

Rex saw Dodo's eyes narrow. "Well, Lauren, this might just be your lucky day! My friend here is a very famous French chef: Raymond … Le … Le… Raymond Le Bleu! Say bonjour to Lauren, Raymond."

Dodo stared hard at Rex; Rex stared blankly at the lights.

"Raymond!" He gave Rex a little kick in the shin. "Bonjour!"

"Uh! Huh? Ummm … bonjour?" said Rex.

"Raymond here can fill in and cook up something fabulous," said Dodo. "And he'll do it for the same fee, even though he's the most famous chef in all of France."

"Really?" Lauren looked delighted. "What a coincidence! You're a lifesaver, Monsieur Le Bleu. Just let me know which ingredients you need."

Lauren hurried away and Rex blinked at Dodo. "But I'm not a chef. And what is France?"

"Look, Rex, I know a business opportunity when I see one. There's money at stake here." He rummaged in his bag, passing Rex a bundle of clothes. "It'll be easy. Just try to remember: you're Raymond Le Bleu and you say 'Bonjour'."

Rex was wide-eyed. "But Mr Dodo, what am I supposed to do when I'm on TV?"

"Food, Rex!" Dodo flapped his wings. "You've got to make them food. And cooking has to come from the heart, so you should make them food that *you* love. Don't worry, it'll be fine – humans eat any old trash."

Rex barely had time to send off his ingredients list before he was manoeuvred in front of bright lights. They made Rex squint.

"OK, everyone, we're live in 3 ... 2 ... 1..."

Bonjour! I am Raymond Le Bleu, a human chef.

Today, I'm going to be cooking food for you. Bonjour!

A good friend of mine said I should cook you what I love to eat.

Well, what I love to eat is Stegosaurus ... but you can't find those in the city!

CHAPTER 10
PREDATORS

Sandra prided herself on being prepared for whatever surprises an investigation might throw her way … but she had to admit, she hadn't been expecting this.

"Mr Rex isn't a chef though, is he?" Anish – who had come over to Sandra's flat to get fully up to speed on the investigation – wrinkled his nose in puzzlement.

"Not as far as I know," said Sandra. "And we know for *sure* he's not called 'Raymond Le Bleu'! Anish—"

"'Flying Pig'," corrected Anish.

"Flying Pig," Sandra continued, "I've got some clues I want to show you."

They made a run for Sandra's investigation HQ, which was the old shed behind the brambles in the communal gardens. Sandra had been archiving evidence there.

"OK, Big Spider – so what are these unusual phenomenomenomina you've seen around Mr Rex?"

(*Author's note: "Phenomena" is one of those words that you can never quite be sure when to stop saying.*)

Sandra pointed to the evidence. "Phenomenonynomona include…"

- Strange noises
- Damage to doors
- Unfashionable dress sense
- An ability to bite through anything
- A diet of snack foods
- A tendency to call people "humans"
- General confusion about everything
- An apparent hatred of tennis

"It's like he's never been to the city before."

Anish picked up the tennis racket Sandra had found in the bin, inspecting the bite mark. "It's like he's never been to the *world* before."

They both stopped and looked at each other.

"You don't think—" said Anish.

"It's the only possible explanation!" said Sandra. "Mr Rex isn't human, he's an ..."

said Sandra and Anish together.

"Do you think he's got a spaceship?" wondered Sandra, peering out of the shed window.

"He must do," said Anish. "How else would he have got to our planet? I suppose he's come to learn about how Earth works – that explains why he's so confused." He started pacing up and down. "What about Mr Foot? Do you think he knows?"

Sandra looked up at Mr Foot's flat. "I imagine he has no idea."

"Where do you think he keeps the ship? Maybe we should search the car park?"

Sandra and Anish ran out of the shed and sprinted across the grass … but they weren't the only ones in the garden. When it was already too late to turn back unseen, Sandra spotted Maddie and the Hannahs coming through the gates towards them.

"Oh, now I understand why you wanted to hang out here," Hannah P told Maddie. "We can have some more fun with the bin-diver."

"What are you guys doing here?" said Sandra, doing her best to ignore Hannah P.

"You told me to stay away from you, Maddie, so why are you coming to my flats?"

"Look, Sandra, I had to—" Maddie started to answer, but Hannah M butted in.

"Hey! I know what will get that bin stink off you… The smell of freshly cut grass!"

Before Sandra knew what was happening, Hannah M had not only tripped her over but also started pulling up fistfuls of grass and stuffing them down the back of Sandra's shirt. "Look, Mads … grass!" Hannah M waved a fist of grass at Maddie, who looked like she was about to speak – but Anish got there first.

"HEY! That's dangerous!" shouted Anish. "What if Sandra catches hay fever?!"

But this only resulted in Hannah P sitting on his legs and putting dandelions in his hair.

"She's surprisingly strong!" Anish wiggled to free himself, as Sandra tried to fend off Hannah M's handfuls of grass. "Are your investigations always this dangerous, Sandra?"

Meanwhile, Rex was nearly back at the flat – but he was dreading telling Bigfoot what had happened at the TV station. He rounded the corner … and was horrified by what he saw.

Predators were attacking the human girl from downstairs! And a boy human, who must be part of her pack.

Rex couldn't let that happen. And he knew a thing or two about predators – including

what to do when someone thought they could
be the new King of the Dinosaurs. He puffed
himself up and stomped towards them, waving
his claws and trying to look big.

Sandra looked up and gasped – and also
accidentally inhaled a daisy – when she saw
Mr Rex, with his huge teeth and dirty chef's
clothes, storming towards them.

"We have to go, now!" shouted Maddie, pulling a Hannah off Sandra.

"It was just a game!" yelled the first Hannah, who was already starting to run.

"They started it!" yelled the other Hannah … and then the girls ran off, leaving Sandra and Anish on the ground – grassy but unharmed.

Mr Rex bent down, so he was at eye level with them, and said, "I have chased away the predators, human children. Did they bite you?"

Sandra looked up at Rex, a little nervous to be talking to an alien. "No bites. Thank you."

"They should look for new hunting grounds now," said Mr Rex. "That's what the Velociraptors used to do, anyway."

"I've watched films about alien invasions with my uncle, Big Spider," Anish told Sandra in a quick whisper. "I know just what to say!"

Sandra frowned at Anish; Mr Rex just looked confused.

"Do you mean Big ... er ... Mr Foot?" said Mr Rex. "Maybe later. I think he's going to be in a bad mood today. Bonjour, hatchlings!"

And with that, Mr Rex stomped off towards the bins.

Sandra could barely contain her excitement. "We just spoke to an ALIEN!"

Not only had she helped to solve a mystery for the first time, but they had made contact with an alien species. Even grown-up investigators hadn't done that!

"So cool!" But Anish's smile looked a little worried. "Seriously though, Sandra, what's going on with Maddie? Everyone knows the Hannahs are the WORST, but I used to think Maddie was nice. Now she's acting like she can't bear to be around us, but also can't stay away. My mum would call that 'contradictory behaviour'."

Sandra shrugged. "I'm as confused as you are."

Anish considered this. "If she's bullying you, you should tell your mum and dad."

Sandra thought about trying to tell Mum and Dad ... but all she could imagine was Larry,

Gary and Barry crying again. "Why are we talking about Maddie when we just met an alien?" she said, deciding to change the subject. "I think you muddled him with all that talk of leaders."

"But did you notice, he let slip that Mr Foot was his leader – so, *he* must be an alien too," said Anish.

Sandra was quietly impressed – Anish had got the hang of this whole investigation business very quickly.

"You're on to something, Flying Pig…" she said. "And we're going to go down in history as the first people to have made contact with alien life – we just need some kind of proof."

"Any ideas on how we go about getting that?" said Anish.

"You know Mrs Mince, who owns our building?" said Sandra. "Well, she has a key to every flat. If you can distract her, I can sneak past and look for Mr Foot's keys."

They wasted no time getting to work – and Anish's enthusiastic distraction worked a treat.

Soon, they would be inside the alien's den.

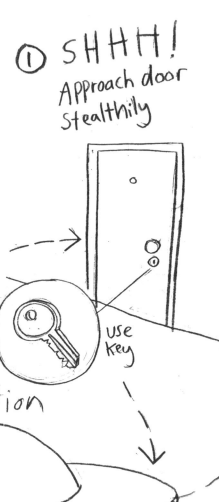

① SHHH! Approach door Stealthily

use key

Assess situation ②

Alien Space Craft

Sofa

Rug

Coffee

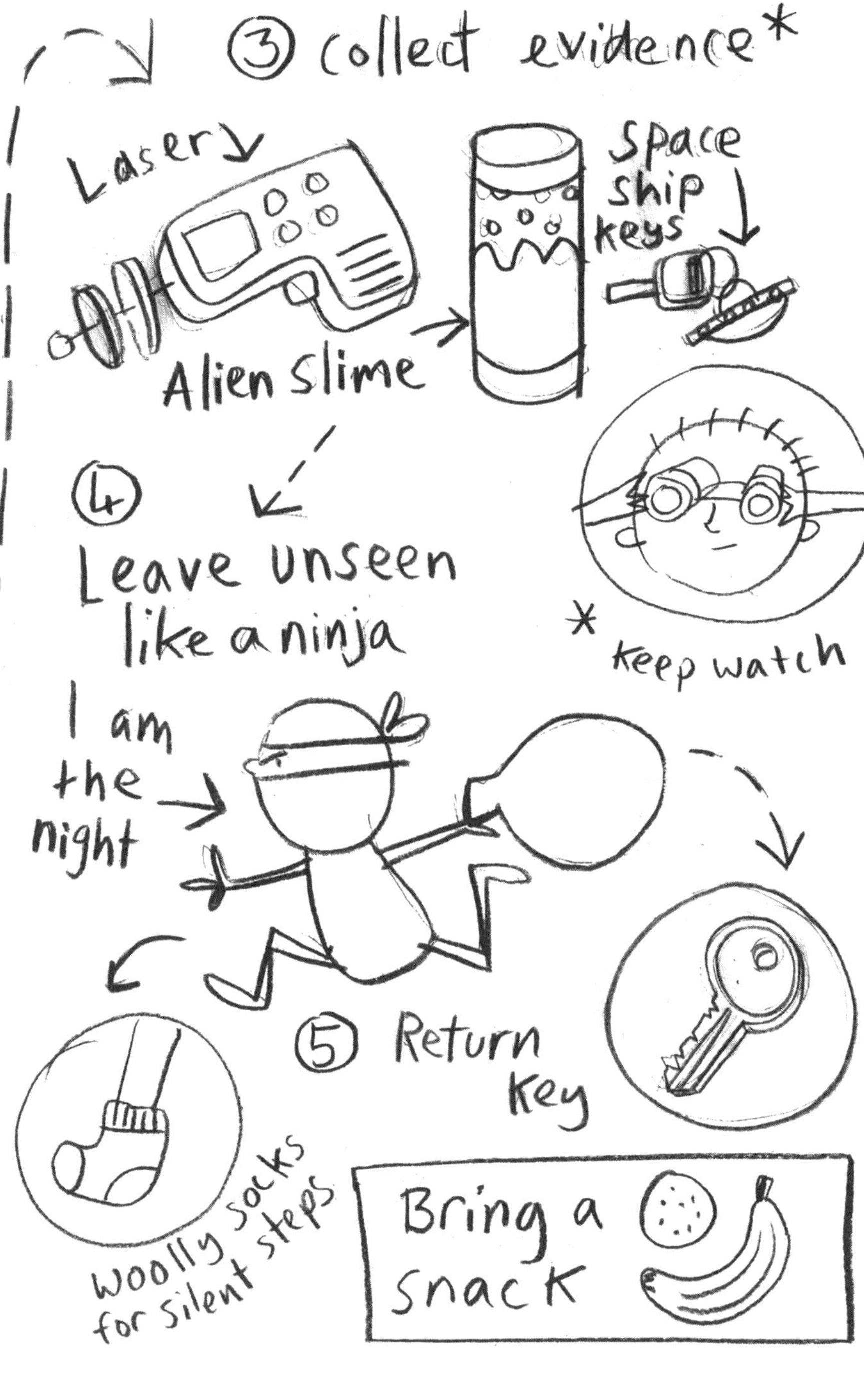

③ collect evidence*

Laser↓

Alien slime

Space ship keys↓

④ Leave unseen like a ninja

* keep watch

I am the night →

⑤ Return Key

woolly socks for silent steps

Bring a snack

CHAPTER 11
NO MORE CHANCES

Rex already knew that he'd messed up his last chance, but it was only when Bigfoot got home that he realized how bad things *really* were.

Bigfoot dropped down to sit on the end of Rex's bed. "This is VERY BAD, Rex. I've never known anyone to get sacked three times in one week… And this last time really takes the biscuit. Do you understand why I'm angry?"

"I didn't take any biscuits," said Rex defensively. "And I didn't bring the messy chef's clothes into the flat."

"No, it's not about those things." Bigfoot's large brow wrinkled into a frown.

"Is it that I made the celebrities messy? I didn't bring them into the flat either."

"No," said Bigfoot, with an irritated huff.

"Is it that I didn't bring you home any of the food?"

"No, no, no, Rex!" Bigfoot leapt up off the bed, raised his hands to his head and grabbed fistfuls of hair in frustration. "It's that you keep acting so … WEIRD! You can't go around talking about Stegosauruses, or trying to feed pop stars sheep covered in lasagne – especially not on national TV!"

"I thought they'd find it fun," said Rex. "But humans are not like dinosaurs… Mr Dodo said he was 'genuinely impressed I found something that humans didn't want to eat'."

"Honestly, I don't think much of Dodo's judgement after this farce." Bigfoot exhaled sharply. "I can't afford to pay for all those Cheez Nubbins by myself – I need help. It's like you're not even trying, Rex."

"I am trying!" Rex pulled the duvet right up to his face, so only his eyes peeped out. "But it's hard when everything is so new. The human world is nothing like the dinosaur world – and if all the humans knew I was a dinosaur, and that I'm new to being human, then it wouldn't seem so weird to them."

"How many TIMES, Rex? Do you seriously want to end up in a zoo? If you ever say a word about being a dinosaur, the humans will be down here with their nets and cages! It's too dangerous."

Bigfoot started stomping around the room. With those feet of his, Bigfoot made Rex's stomping sound like that of a mouse in slippers.

Rex scrunched up the duvet in his claws. "It just doesn't make sense. If humans make movies about dinosaurs  … and have dinosaurs on their T-shirts and office mugs … and make little tiny dino-toys … and even have dinosaur-shaped pasta … why wouldn't everyone be happy that I'm a dinosaur?"

Rex was starting to feel angry with Bigfoot now – he really was trying his best, but nothing ever seemed to be good enough. Plucking up his courage, he seized one of his dinosaur toys and pointed it at Bigfoot.

"I think you're afraid, Bigfoot. It's like you don't know how to be your real self any more."

"Of COURSE I'm afraid! You don't understand anything about humans, or about Being Human – and your behaviour is putting everyone in danger. Me, you, Dodo and even Nessy!"

Bigfoot was getting louder: his nostrils flared and he flung his big yeti arms in the air.

"Have you even seen one of those dinosaur movies? The dinosaurs eat EVERYONE and the humans all run away. That's what they think you're like!"

Every hair on Bigfoot's particularly hairy body was standing on end, making him look even bigger than he usually did.

"We had it all sorted until you got here, Rex – we were safe! My life would have been so much easier if I had just left you in that museum."

With a last stamp of his foot, Bigfoot stormed out of the room … and then, out of the flat.

All of a sudden, Rex felt sick and exhausted. He missed the prehistoric world: he missed the forests, and the swamps, and the volcanoes, and the Stegosauruses, and even the Velociraptors. But these things that he actually understood were gone now.

Rex gathered up all his dino-toys in his tiny arms and started to sniffle…

And that's when the human girl burst out of the wardrobe.

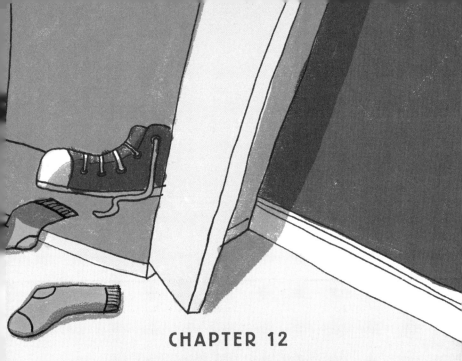

CHAPTER 12

MYSTERY SOLVED

R ex was so shocked that he stopped crying. "I didn't know small humans lived in those!" he said, dropping his little dinos behind him as he hurried over to the wardrobe. "Bigfoot told me that's where we keep socks and things. Sorry if I filled your house with my underwear."

"OH MY GOSH! You're a dinosaur?" The human girl sprang up. "A real-life T-REX? I thought you guys were extinct."

Rex went from confused to very worried. Bigfoot would be so angry if he realized a human had found out about Rex, and he didn't think Bigfoot could get any angrier without accidentally stomping the flat down.

"Please don't put me in a zoo!" said Rex. "I'm not scary and I won't eat you – I eat Cheez Nubbins, not people."

The human girl looked surprised. "Scared? I'm not scared, this is the most awesome thing that has ever happened!" She beamed at him. "My name's Sandra, by the way. I can't believe it: dinosaurs are the BEST!"

It took a moment for Rex to understand.

"You mean you … *like* dinosaurs?"

"Yes!" Sandra nodded, telling him again, but this time more gently: "They're the best."

Rex had known it all along: of COURSE humans loved dinosaurs! How else could you possibly explain the dinosaur-shaped pasta?

"And you can talk!" said Sandra. "Can all dinosaurs talk?"

Rex thought about this. "In prehistoric times, we used to just roar at each other – Bigfoot taught me speaking. I think I'm the only one."

"This just gets more exciting!" Sandra did a happy little jump, then suddenly called over her shoulder, "Anish, it's safe! You can come out."

Muffled shouts and banging noises came from Rex's chest of drawers.

"Oh, yeah," said Sandra, before heading over to the drawers and pulling out the bottom one to reveal the human boy from before.

"How many of you are in here? Do all humans move in herds?" said Rex.

"It's just the two of us," said the boy, untangling himself from Rex's shorts. "I'm Anish." He shook Rex's claw vigorously and gave him a big, excited grin. "I've never met a dinosaur before. Can I have your autograph?"

"Autowho?" said Rex.

"And is Mr Foot some kind of dinosaur too? Or is he an alien?" asked Anish.

"He's something called a 'yeti'." Rex frowned. "Apparently, humans don't like them either."

Anish's face lit up. "A REAL yeti?! I love yetis! I've seen all the photos of them."

Rex was starting to wonder why Bigfoot had been so worried about humans: these two seemed just fine. "How did you get in my room? Do you live with us now?"

"We still live with our families," said Sandra. "But I might have, sort of, *borrowed* the spare keys from Mrs Mince, so we could look for alien stuff in your flat."

"Now we know why we didn't find anything," said Anish. "We should have been looking for DINOSAUR stuff."

Rex's face dropped. "The thing is, I'm not supposed to be a dinosaur any more, I'm meant to be a human. But Bigfoot says I'm really bad at it and then he left, and now I…"

Rex started to tear up again, but – through the waterfall of prehistoric snot – he managed to more or less tell Sandra and Anish everything.

"… and I still don't understand so much of the human world! There are too many mysteries to solve. And I can't make ANY of these human machines work properly!"

Rex picked up a pencil, some scissors and a glove, and thrust them up in the air.

Sandra narrowed her eyes. "Well, mysteries are kind of my thing. How about we help? We're actual humans, after all, so we're pretty much experts on human stuff."

"Yep!" said Anish. "I can use at least two out of three of those 'machines'."

"Two out of three?" said Sandra.

"Those scissors look sharp," said Anish.

Rex started to feel hopeful for the first time since the TV show. "You'll HELP?"

"Of course! And let's start with how *this* works," said Sandra, brandishing the pencil.

CHAPTER 13
ALL BY MYSELF

While all this was going on, Bigfoot had been stomping around the city streets.

Usually when he felt this bad, Bigfoot would do one of the "city" things he loved – like going to a gallery while wearing his arty scarf, or getting a double-flat-extra-Peruvian-tall-white from his favourite coffee place.

But Bigfoot just didn't feel like doing any of that now.

What was he supposed to do about Rex? Bigfoot was sure he had been in the right: Rex didn't make a very good human, and he was ruining the extremely human life Bigfoot had worked so hard to create.

Then again, things certainly hadn't been boring since Rex had turned up, had they?

And if Bigfoot was honest with himself, he was bored of living on his own. Having someone around the flat to talk to, especially about how strange the human world could be, had been kind of ... nice.

Had he been a bit mean to Rex, saying he wished he'd never found him? He supposed Rex was actually trying – he was just trying in all the wrong directions.

Maybe I should try to be nicer, thought Bigfoot, *and make Rex feel more at home.*

I could get Rex his own arty scarf, and we could go to the gallery together... Or maybe Rex would like to go for a fancy coffee somewhere?

Or... *Maybe* he should try doing things that Rex might like, not just Bigfoot things. Rex seemed to enjoy running around chasing stuff – maybe they could play football? Or, they could go to the botanic gardens ... they seemed a bit like a prehistoric forest.

Bigfoot made up his mind: he would go home and make things right with Rex. He hurried all the way back, the pavement shaking as he stomped – but when Bigfoot finally stepped inside the flat, he was horrified by what he saw.

"Rex, what have you DONE?!" Bigfoot had never been more afraid of anything than the two children sat on his living room floor.

"Hello, Mr Foot – it's me, Sandra!" As she spoke, Bigfoot suddenly recognized the girl who lived downstairs... The one who was always asking questions. "And this is my best friend, Anish." He gazed around the room in horror, his eyes falling on the human boy who gave Bigfoot a thumbs up.

Bigfoot made a gagging sound – there was a real possibility that he might be sick.

Unphased, Sandra continued: "It's nice to meet you properly, Mr Foot." She got up and shook his hand. "Or, should I say, 'Bigfoot'.

Hi, Mr Foot.

We've just been showing Rex how pencils
work… And he showed us round the flat.
I really like your collection of French films.
Le Chat is my favourite."

"Yes, it's a genre-defining classic," said
Bigfoot distractedly – but then he refocused.
"PLEASE DON'T CALL THE ZOO! Rex, we
have to run."

Bigfoot tried to grab Rex and drag him towards the door – but he didn't budge.

"It's OK, Bigfoot! They're humans, but not bad ones... Just let us explain."

Rex, Sandra and Anish told Bigfoot about what had happened.

"So, we don't want to put either of you in a zoo," Sandra finished. "We want to help."

"Your secret is safe with us," said Anish. "I know loads of secrets."

"You do?" said Sandra, curious. "Like what?"

"I'm not telling, because I'm an excellent secret-keeper."

"So, you see ... Mr Foot? Are you OK?"

Bigfoot was feeling faint. Anish got him a paper bag to breathe into before they carried on.

"We think we can help with Rex's job issues, too," said Sandra. "There's been a recent opening which could be perfect for Rex."

"Yes, it would involve lots of running about and being loud," put in Anish.

"I really want to try again," said Rex. "Can I go for the interview, Bigfoot? Please, please, please ... please?"

Bigfoot put down his paper bag. The shock was passing, and actually these human children – with their knowledge of classic cinema – didn't seem that scary after all.

Could he trust them? It would be so useful to finally have some real humans on their side.

"I suppose it's worth a try," he said at last.

"Amazing!" said Sandra quickly. "You should apply right away, Rex. I've got a feeling this job is going to be just perfect."

CHAPTER 14

TIME FOR SCHOOL

Rex found himself in the head teacher's office at Lower Patterson Primary School.

"I very much enjoy running around, I have a loud voice and I know exactly what to do with pencils," he said firmly.

Mr Alfreds seemed to think about this. "Well … that's more than I can say for the last PE teacher. Do you have any strong opinions concerning guinea pigs?"

Rex gave Mr Alfreds a blank look. "I've genuinely never thought about them."

"Perfect! When would you be available?"

"Right away," said Rex, giving Mr Alfreds his best smile.

The head teacher clapped his hands together. "Well, Mr Rex, I like your gumption and I like your availability. You're hired!" He shook Rex's claw. "That's a good strong grip."

Rex was thrilled, if also a little concerned that "gumption" might be that stuff which came out of his nose when he cried.

Because Bigfoot had picked out a human sports outfit for Rex earlier that morning, he was able to start his PE lessons right away. What's more, Rex soon found being a dinosaur and being a PE teacher went hand in hand.

OK, kids, let's get running and roaring!

You'll never catch a herbivore standing still!

Is this going to be another guinea pig situation?

ROAR like a T-Rex

STOMP! like a Spinosaurus!

Be the Giganotosaurus!

Rex's lessons were a huge success. In just a week, his dinosaur-themed activities turned PE from being the most dreaded lesson in Lower Patterson Primary, to the most popular.

Everyone was delighted. Well … nearly everyone.

There's something I don't like about the new PE teacher.

Later that week, Rex was on playground duty – and paying close attention, in case the children started displaying too much predator-like behaviour and he had to step in.

His concentration was broken when Sandra tugged on his sleeve. "How's it going, Rex?" she asked. "Oh – I mean, *Mr* Rex."

"It's great!" said Rex. "The kids are really fun, everyone is nice to me in the staff room and I can drink as much coffee as I like. Though I'm very careful not to make too much. Even better, Bigfoot is SO pleased with me!"

He scrunched up his eyes in joy and clasped his claws together.

"He says I'm 'really contributing' and that my new athleisure outfits are 'very human'."

"All the kids are talking about how much they like your lessons. Even the Year Sixes!"

Sandra came closer, and whispered excitedly, "You're everyone's new favourite teacher, human or dinosaur!"

Rex glowed with pride. He'd been doing this job for DAYS, and not only had he avoided getting fired, but he was actually good at it.

It was time to blow the whistle for the end of break, and Sandra ran off to join her class. While everyone filed back into the building, Rex popped into the staff toilets. He checked to see if there were any feet under the stall doors and, when he was sure it was empty, he took off his glasses...

And looked in the mirror at his dinosaur face, smiling at himself with his pointy teeth.

He'd made friends with two actual, real humans. Maybe he could make friends with them ALL, and then they wouldn't even care if they found out he was a dinosaur?

But there wasn't time to think about that now. He had to take volleyball practice next … so he'd have to learn what volleyball was.

Finally, things seemed to be going Rex's way. And maybe everything really would have been all right – if Rex actually *had* been alone in those toilets.

CHAPTER 15
SPORTS DAY

The biggest test of Rex's PE teacher skills was fast approaching – it was nearly Sports Day, and Rex would be in charge.

A few days before, Rex caught up with Sandra and Anish to ask what a "Sports Day" was. They explained it was pretty much just an all-day PE lesson, pretending to be fun. On top of that, as the PE teacher, Rex was responsible for organizing everything – which made him nervous. Last time Rex had been in charge of anything, he'd ruined swimming.

"Everyone loves your dinosaur PE lessons," Sandra reassured him. "Just do that, but … *bigger*, and with medals at the end. Hey…" Her eyes lit up. "Why don't we all DRESS UP like dinosaurs?"

"That's a great idea! Oh, and it's important to also let the parents do some races," said Anish. "They act like they don't want to, but they're very competitive. My uncle *always* enters."

Rex relaxed a bit. Sports Day didn't sound too hard. "Will your family come and watch, too?" he asked Sandra.

Sandra looked at her feet. "Maybe, but Dad says that it's hard to go anywhere when you've got three babies in tow. He says they'll be able

to go out again when the babies are eighteen …
and that's not before Sports Day."

"I'll be there, cheering you on." Rex gave
Sandra a pat on the shoulder with a claw. "But
quietly, because teachers aren't supposed to
have favourites and I'm a professional."

"I can't wait for your very professional
Dinosaur Sports Day," Sandra said, and gave
Rex a pat on the back in return.

When Sports Day finally came around, Rex put his plans into action. He found that being in charge came naturally when he actually knew what he was supposed to be doing – especially with Sandra and Anish there, lending a hand.

To kick things off, Rex gathered the parents, children and teachers on the sports field ... ready to open Sports Day by leading all the children in a mighty dinosaur roar.

The only snag was that the volleyballs had gone missing.

"Oh, Nubbins!" said Rex. "We need those for the first event, 'Avoid the Asteroid Shower'."

"I think there are some spares in the sports hall cupboard," said Sandra, who was so excited about Dinosaur Sports Day that she'd been in her T-Rex costume since breakfast.

"I'll go and tell everyone that you'll only be a moment," said Anish, before he flapped away, waving his papier-mâché Pterodactyl wings.

As Rex hurried across the playground, closely followed by Sandra, he bumped into someone.

"Bigfoot!" cried Rex. "What are you doing here? Shouldn't you be at work? Or did you make too much coffee, and they had to let you go?"

"I took the day off," said Bigfoot – and Rex was sure his flatmate had never taken a day off before in his life. Then he pulled Rex into a hug. "This is your big day, Rex. You've been doing so well, and I wanted to support you..." He stepped back. "Plus I'm a big fan of egg and spoon races, both amateur and professional."

"I'm really glad you're here!" Rex felt so proud he thought he might burst. "I can show you what a good job I've been doing."

"It's so nice you came, Bigfoot," said Sandra. "I wish my mum and dad could have—" But the end of her sentence was drowned out by the revving of an engine, and the screech of tyres. A black van streaked around the corner onto the playground.

"FREEZE!" said a very loud voice. "This is the ZOO!"

Before Rex understood what was happening,
men in uniforms were piling out of a van labelled
ZOO S.W.A.T. – and then, they were on him.

Detain the dinosaur!

Bigfoot! HELP!

Bigfoot
didn't stand a
chance either.

For a moment, Sandra was stunned – but there was no way she was going to let them take Rex and Mr Foot without a fight.

Her efforts came to nothing, however, and Sandra was forced to watch as the van screeched away with Rex and Bigfoot inside ... leaving her all alone.

Or so she thought – until Maddie stepped out from her hiding place.

CHAPTER 16

WHATEVER HAPPENED TO MADDIE

It was the first time Sandra had seen Maddie without the Hannahs for weeks. At first, she felt a jolt of relief at the sight of her old friend – but when Sandra's brain kicked in, she knew something wasn't right about this.

"Maddie, did you see that? They kidnapped Rex and Bigfoot! I mean … Mr Rex, the PE teacher, and my neighbour, Mr—"

Maddie came right up close to Sandra, and hissed through clenched teeth, "Drop the act, Sandra! I know who Mr Rex really is. Or should I say … *what* he really is."

OK, this definitely doesn't sound good, thought Sandra. But maybe Maddie could be persuaded to help.

"There'll be time to explain, I promise," said Sandra. "But right now, we need to do something – we have to call someone, like a teacher..."

Maddie wasn't panicking like Sandra. She was still and serious. "No we don't, Sandra. This is exactly what I wanted to happen."

Sandra stared at her, stunned. "You mean – YOU did this? But why?"

"I know things now, Sandra. Things you don't." Maddie fixed Sandra with an intense stare. "I looked on Mum's ePad. It turns out there are loads of videos about the kind of mysteries we used to 'investigate' – but it's not what we thought. They're not exciting or interesting ... they're dangerous.

There are aliens who want to hurt us ...

monsters who want to take our homes ...

and our money …

Ghosts want my money! So I keep it in jars.

and even our pets.

BIGFOOT SWALLOWED MY KITTEN! I MISS FLUFFY!

You shouldn't be messing with these things," she continued, "because there's no room for monsters in a world that's safe for humans like us. *That's* why I called the zoo about 'Mr Rex'."

Sandra's body felt weak as she took a step back from Maddie.

All this time she had been desperate to get close to Maddie again – and now that they were finally talking, every single word that came out of Maddie's mouth felt completely wrong.

"What makes you think the people in those videos were telling the truth?" Sandra asked. "Can any of them prove they've actually *met* an alien or a ghost?"

"It was on the internet, Sandra," said Maddie, "so it's got to be real."

"Well, what about evidence?" said Sandra. "We were always looking for evidence, when we did our investigations."

"Those were little kids' games." Maddie rolled her eyes. "I know what the grown-ups know, now – and when you act as if those creatures are your *friends*, you're putting everyone in danger."

"But *I* know Rex. And he IS my friend."

Maddie's scowl deepened. "He's a T-rex, Sandra, not a puppy. You should be grateful I've saved you from that monster... And I hope this teaches you not to mess with things you don't understand." She gave Sandra a cold, hard smile, then stormed away.

Sandra felt so angry inside … but her face didn't seem to have got the message, because it just felt like she was about to cry.

But before any tears could fall, Sandra spotted Anish running across the playground.

"How long does it take to get some volleyballs?" he puffed – then, as he paused to catch his breath, he frowned. "Where's Mr Rex?"

Sandra held back the tears, took a deep breath and explained everything. By the time she was finished, Anish's mouth was wide open.

"They just … took them? What are we supposed to do? I think I need to tell my mum."

"No, hang on," said Sandra slowly, "don't do that." Her anger was steadily turning into a plan.

Anish was thinking too. "None of the grown-ups will believe us if we tell them the zoo kidnapped the PE teacher because he's really a dinosaur, will they?"

"Exactly," said Sandra. "But I have an idea. Do you have a bus pass?"

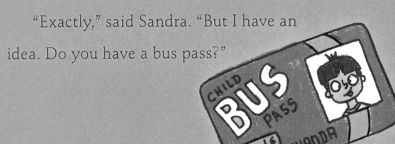

CHAPTER 17
THE ZOO

Even though the thing he had dreaded most had come to pass, Rex thought Bigfoot looked oddly calm.

They had been taken across the city to a building marked **The Zoo**, and caged in a hangar where visitors weren't allowed to go; a place where fluorescent lights buzzed and something kept dripping on Rex's head.

Rex felt terrible. He had tried so hard to be a good human, but even when things seemed to be going well, he had somehow managed to mess it all up.

What was worse was that he'd dragged Bigfoot into it too.

"Bigfoot, I'm so sorry," Rex whispered. "You were right all along – and I've got us into so much trouble."

Bigfoot let out a big sigh and looked at Rex through the bars.

"Rex, this isn't your fault. You did your best – we're all just doing our best – but we got rumbled anyway." Bigfoot rubbed his hands over his head as he thought, messing up his hair. "Do you know what? I think I knew all along that someone would find out in the end. Lies always get found out."

Rex was feeling a lot of feelings: more than he ever had back in prehistoric times. His nose was filling with gumption, but he wasn't sure if it was because he was sad at being trapped in a zoo, or happy that Bigfoot didn't hate him.

Bigfoot stuck a big hand between the bars and took hold of one of Rex's little foreclaws.

"No touching!" shouted one of the guards.

"You can't keep us here like animals," Bigfoot snapped back. "I'm a Senior Printer Operator, you know!"

"I'm forbidden from talking to the animals, and that includes abominable snowmen," replied the guard.

"We prefer the term 'yeti'," said Bigfoot.
"Or 'sasquatch', depending on where
you're from."

"An animal is an animal," said the guard.

Bigfoot was getting riled up. "I've read all
the major French philosophers in the original

language. NO ONE is going to try and tell me I'm an animal!"

"Bonjour," Rex put in defiantly.

Before the first guard could respond, another came round the corner carrying two bowls of brown pellets in goop.

"Feeding time!" yelled the new guard, who slid the bowls through the bars.

Bigfoot gave his bowl a disdainful look. "This is the food you give dogs."

"It's standard issue bulk animal feed," said the new guard.

Rex gave it a sniff. "It smells like the floor."

"I demand to be treated with respect and fed human food!" Bigfoot picked up his bowl of dog food and offered it back through the bars.

"Do you have any Cheez Nubbins?" asked Rex hopefully.

"I think there are some in the vending machine…" said the second guard.

"Don't you go anywhere near that vending machine!" interrupted the first. "They'll eat the food provided, and no mouthy snowman is going to tell me any different."

Rex was getting quite good, now, at noticing when Bigfoot had lost his temper – and from the way Bigfoot's fur was sticking up, Rex was concerned he might never find it again.

"If you call me a snowman one more time—" Bigfoot growled.

"This is one of the most secure containment facilities in the country," said the guard. "What exactly are you going to do … *snowman?*"

Bigfoot decided to demonstrate.

And before the guard could react, all of the

lights went out.

MAYDAY! MAYDAY! ANIMAL ATTACK IN PROGRESS!
HAS THERE BEEN A BREAK-OUT IN THE TIGER ENCLOSURE?
WAAAAAAAAAAHHHH!
THE DINOSAUR MUST HAVE CALLED FOR BACK-UP!
I THINK ONE BIT ME!

EVACUATE THE AREA!

DINOSAUR ATTACK!

CHAPTER 18

DINOSAUR ATTACK

In the dark, it was absolute chaos. Rex hadn't heard so much roaring, screeching, barking and crunching for several million years.

Just when he was wondering if he'd somehow found his way back to the Cretaceous Period, something familiar came rushing out of the darkness.

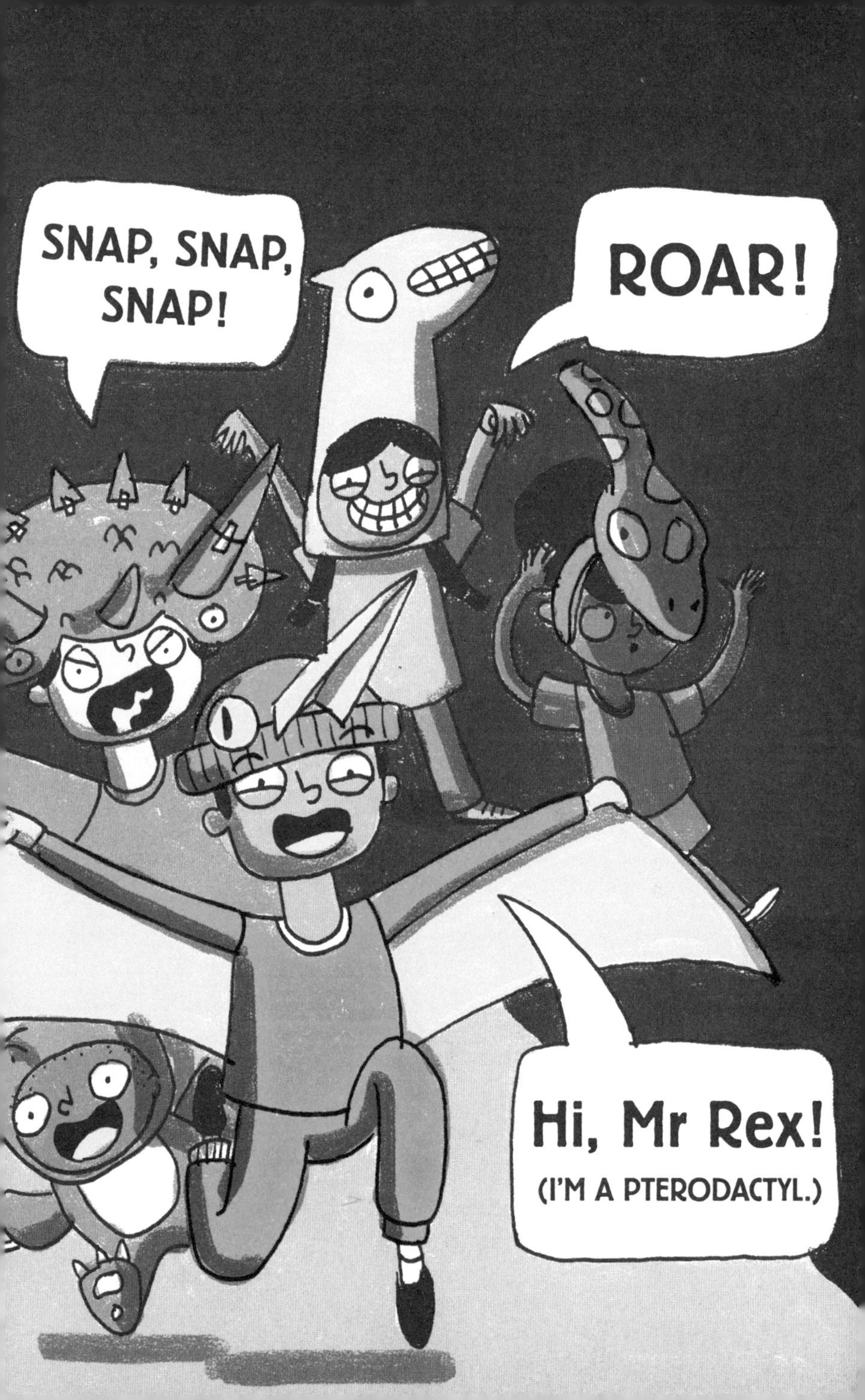
SNAP, SNAP, SNAP!
ROAR!
Hi, Mr Rex!
(I'M A PTERODACTYL.)

And then a *very* familiar dinosaur
popped up in front of Rex's cage.

Sandra!

"Yes, it's me!" Sandra, who'd stolen
the guards' keys during the confusion, set
to work unlocking their cages. "Come on,
let's get out of here – I'll fetch the others."

DINOSAURS! RETREAT!

In the dark, the guards couldn't tell the difference between a real Pterodactyl and Anish wearing papier-mâché wings, so they fled right out of the main doors. Year 4, Rex and Bigfoot made their escape out the back.

When everyone was safely out of the hangar, they found a hiding place and began jumping around in celebration.

"Incredible! I used to know real dinosaurs that weren't nearly as convincing," said Rex.

"We learned it all from your lessons, Mr Rex," said Anish.

"Tyrannosaurus ROAR!" said Jade from 4B.

"Spinosaurus STOMP!" said Nadia from 4B.

"*BE* the Giganotosaurus!" said Ethan from 2F (who wasn't supposed to be there, but had tagged along with his big sister, Nadia, from 4B).

"No one wanted their favourite PE teacher locked up," said Sandra with a wink.

"Yeah, what if Mrs Libson came back?" said Anish, and everyone shuddered. "We snuck out while the teachers were looking for you – and we took the bus all by ourselves."

Bigfoot looked concerned, but Rex clapped his claws in delight – and Year 4 (and Ethan) started cheering again.

Sandra leaned in so that the rest of the class couldn't hear, and whispered, "What are we going to do next? It was Maddie who called the zoo … she knows about you. I don't think you're safe in the city any more."

Rex saw her eyes start to water, and the feeling of success drained out of him.

"Sandra's right," he told Bigfoot. "Our disguises won't work now. Will we have to move to another city, far away, and start again? There are other cities, aren't there, Bigfoot?"

"Yes, lots," said Bigfoot, but he seemed distracted.

Sandra couldn't stop the tears now. "But you're my friends! I don't want you to go!"

Rex didn't want to go either. The human world had been scary, but now he had a home, a job, new friends … *and* Cheez Nubbins.

But he couldn't let Bigfoot end up in the zoo. They'd just have to find a new home together.

"I'm going to miss you all so much," he said. "We never really 'did' friends in the Cretaceous Period – what with all the eating each other – so it's been great to have some."

Rex pulled Sandra into a hug. But then his attention shifted back to Bigfoot, because he was behaving in a very un-Bigfoot way: undoing his tie, before flinging it to the ground.

"No! We can't do this any more! We've tried running, hiding and being scared, and it didn't work." Bigfoot pushed between Rex and Sandra, and spoke urgently, "You've made me think, Rex. I don't want to leave this city – but I don't want to pretend to be a human any more. It's time to show all these humans that we deserve to be treated with respect."

Rex was astonished. "That sounds brilliant! But how are we going to do that?"

Sandra wiped her face with her costume and looked up at Bigfoot. "I think we can make enough people see sense... We just need to go back to Sports Day."

"All right, Sandra," said Bigfoot. "But we should pick up a few friends on the way."

"Great!" said Sandra. "Um, do either of you have enough money for the bus home?"

CHAPTER 19
SPORTS DAY AGAIN

The assorted crowd of children and creatures strode onto the sports field – to see quite a scene unfolding.

"I think I'd rather take my chances with the zoo guards," said Anish, and Sandra saw what he meant. Furious parents were gathered around the head teacher, all speaking at once.

"What do you MEAN, the whole of Year Four – and Ethan – are missing?" said Anish's mum.

"And when is the parents' race?!" said Nadia from 4B and Ethan from 2F's stepdad, who was doing stretches. "I've been in training all year."

At the back of the crowd, Sandra spotted a triple-buggy ... and two grown-ups.

"Mum! Dad!" Sandra ran over to them.

"Sandra Jane Shellman! *Where* have you been?" said Mum.

"I thought you weren't coming," said Sandra.

"We couldn't miss this," said Dad. "You seemed so excited this morning."

Sandra flung her arms around them. "I've got so much to tell you," she began – but before she could get any further, Rex had ascended to the podium with a megaphone.

Rex felt like a whole flock of Pterodactyls was flapping about in his stomach, and his claws had started to feel clammy.

He thought about running away ... but then he spotted Bigfoot in the crowd, who gave him a thumbs up.

"Hello? Is this on?" Rex spoke into the megaphone. "Hello, human parents, children and teachers! It's me, Mr Rex, the PE teacher. I have an important announcement to make."

"Is it time for the parents' race?" shouted Nadia and Ethan's stepdad.

"Um ... no. But it's just as important," Rex continued bravely. "I want to tell you ... that I love working here.

I'm new to this city and you've all been so welcoming and kind."

Rex paused to look at the faces in the crowd, which seemed more puzzled than kind, currently, but he grasped the megaphone tighter and carried on.

"I hope you all think I've been a good teacher. I want to keep doing that – but I need to be honest with you first." Rex removed his glasses. "Because I'm NOT a human…"

I'M A DINOSAUR.

He held his breath and waited to see how everyone would react.

Then Bigfoot started clapping furiously.

"Bravo, Rex! Bravo!" He was jumping up and down, making the ground shake.

The children's reactions were equally enthusiastic.

"I've always wanted to meet a dinosaur!" said Arthur from 4C.

"Can we get a triceratops for Year Two?" asked Ethan from 2F.

"Do you think he'll want to appear on my MeTube channel?" asked Asmita from 5R.

But Rex spotted one child who didn't seem impressed. Maddie was tugging at her parents' sleeves and pointing at Rex – and all three looked furious.

"This is unacceptable!" shrieked Maddie's mum. "A dinosaur in a school? It's not safe, or … or educational! What if he eats a high-achieving child?!" She grabbed Maddie protectively.

Her words stung: Rex hadn't eaten a single human. Why would anyone think that?

"I am not going to eat people! Just lasagne and Nubbins," he said, his voice wobbling. "Humans are my friends."

Maddie's dad wasn't going to let this pass without having HIS say. "This area has a certain … quality to it. We have a branch of Harknell and Lefroy's, for goodness' sake!

227

How can a prehistoric MONSTER contribute to our community?"

Rex didn't know what to say. He moved his mouth about, trying to find the right words.

"Actually, undercover creatures are already playing a part in the community." Bigfoot stepped forward. "I'm Brian Foot, AKA Bigfoot, and I've been living and working here for years. I'm a six-time BusinessCorp employee of the month ... and I'm also a yeti."

Bigfoot threw his glasses over his shoulder, before adding, "I'm ALSO short-sighted, so I might regret that."

Rex gave a gasp: Bigfoot!

He'll REALLY show them all, he thought. *Bigfoot's even more human than the humans are.*

"Brian? Brian Foot!" said Anish's uncle. "He's in my spin class."

"And my book club," said Jade's mum.

"And he lives in our building," said Sandra's mum. "He's a very good neighbour – he never complains about the boys crying, and he also puts the bins out."

"And if Brian's all right," said Sandra's dad, "then Mr Rex is probably fine … even if they are yeti-sauruses, or whatever."

Bigfoot gave Rex another little thumbs up. Maybe the school was going to accept them – yeti, dinosaur or otherwise?

Maddie seemed to have other ideas, though. She ran up onto the podium and grabbed the megaphone from Rex.

"Don't let them fool you! These creatures are dangerous – I've seen it on the internet—"

A new voice interrupted her. "Actually, I'm the opposite of dangerous. I've saved several of your lives, at one time or another." Rex saw Nessy step – or rather, shimmy – out of the crowd. "And I'm nae human either:

I'm some kind of … lake-thingy." She waved a flipper vaguely. "To be honest, I'm not sure exactly what kind of creature I am. But I DO know I am a braw lifeguard."

"And me!" Mr Dodo waddled forwards and hopped his way onto

Rex's head. "You lot eat at my restaurant every day! And I'm a dodo." He flung off his glasses, which hit Maddie's dad in the forehead. "That's right: I'm a delicious dodo, but you can't eat me because I'm a valuable member of the local business community!"

The parents began to murmur among themselves, until another voice piped up.

"Look..." It was Nadia and Ethan's stepdad. "We like all of these people, don't we? So why don't we just agree it's fine – and then we can get on with the parents' race?"

Maddie and her family looked fit to burst.

"That's absurd!" shouted Maddie's dad. "You're all being ridiculous!"

"Well!" Mr Alfreds also started to splutter. "I'm not sure what the regulations are about having a dinosaur on the staff, I'd have to talk to the governors…"

"PLEASE, Mr Alfreds!" shouted Anish – and all of the other children, and quite a few of the parents, joined in.

"Think about it, Alfreds!" said Anish's mum. "If you sack ANOTHER PE teacher,

the school will get a reputation. We've all heard about the poor guinea pig."

There were noises of agreement from the

parents, who *had* all heard about the poor guinea pig.

Mr Alfreds' shoulders dropped and, to Rex's amazement, he looked defeated. "I suppose ... perhaps ... on this occasion ... we could probably make an exception."

Another cheer went up, and Rex nearly got carried away with all the excitement – but then he spotted something in the crowd. Maddie, followed closely by the Hannahs, was pushing her way towards Sandra, who was herself distracted by the cheering.

Maddie grabbed one of Sandra's arms, the Hannahs grabbed the other, and together they started pulling her towards the playground.

"Look what you've done, Sandra," Rex heard Maddie hiss. "If you like monsters so much, I'm going to call the zoo and tell them you're some kind of were-rabbit – and then you can spend time caged up with those creatures!"

Rex certainly wasn't going to let *that* happen.

"Stay away from my friend!" He stomped over as fast as he could, the ground shaking beneath him, then loomed over Maddie. "Now the truth is out, Maddie: I'm a T-rex. And do you know what us T-rexes do best?"

Maddie and the Hannahs just stared.

"We ..."

EPILOGUE

"Welcome to our first ever official Undercover Creatures Movie Night!" said Bigfoot, as Rex handed around the Cheez Nubbins. "Tonight we're watching *Le Chat* – as chosen by honorary creature, Sandra."

"I've heard that it's a genre-defining classic!" said Anish, as he settled down with a bowl of popcorn.

Bigfoot gave him a smile, then continued his speech: "But first, I've prepared a short presentation on French cinema!"

Everyone groaned, and before he had time to reach for his laptop, Nessy handed Bigfoot a family-sized packet of Nubbins.

"Maybe after the film, eh, Biggie?" she said, and pressed a button on the remote.

When the film began to play, Sandra leaned over to Rex. "I'm so glad all the parents and teachers agreed you could stay," she whispered. "Mr Alfreds was right: good PE teachers are hard to find."

"It's brilliant! I'm just sad that we had to tell everyone to keep it quiet," said Rex. "I wish we could tell every human in the world!"

"Let's not get ahead of ourselves, young Rex," said Dodo, from his seat in front of Rex. "I've had more than enough excitement... And we've ALL got jobs to be doing, without a bunch of curious humans getting under our feet."

"Sssh! Stop talking over the film," whispered Bigfoot. "It's about to be the bit with the cat!"

As Rex settled down to watch the film, he couldn't help but let his thoughts drift...

A bit of Rex would always miss the forests and swamps and Stegosauruses of prehistoric times. But now he had a place to stay, a job, and more friends than he could count (Bigfoot never did teach him numbers).

Even if he could, Rex wouldn't want to go back.

THE END

ABOUT
THE AUTHOR

Elys Dolan makes books for children
about everything from seagull detectives to
capitalist bunny rabbits and weasels plotting
world domination. She was shortlisted
for the Waterstones Children's Book Prize
for *Weasels*, won the inaugural STEAM
Children's Book Prize for *How the Borks
Became* and the prestigious Lollies Prize
for *Mr Bunny's Chocolate Factory*. She is also
a lecturer on the MA in Children's Book
Illustration at the Cambridge School of Art.

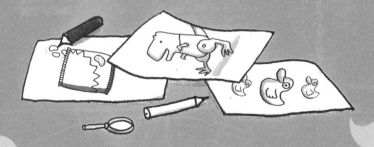